Isabelle
the Ice Dance Fairy

For Catlin Kennedy,
who's full of fairy magic

Special thanks to Narinder Dhami

No part of this work may be reproduced, stored in a retrieval system,
or transmitted in any form or by any means, electronic, mechanical,
photocopying, recording, or otherwise, without written permission
of the publisher. For information regarding permission, write to
Rainbow Magic Limited c/o HIT Entertainment,
830 South Greenville Avenue, Allen, TX 75002-3320.

ISBN-10: 0-545-10623-0
ISBN-13: 978-0-545-10623-8

18 17 16 15 14 13   14 15 16 17/0

Printed in the U.S.A.   40

First Scholastic Printing, May 2009

Isabelle
the Ice Dance Fairy

by Daisy Meadows

SCHOLASTIC INC.

New York Toronto London Auckland Sydney
Mexico City New Delhi Hong Kong Buenos Aires

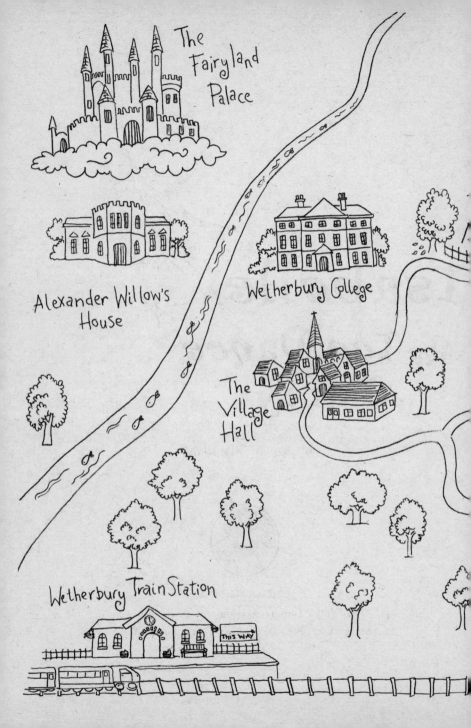

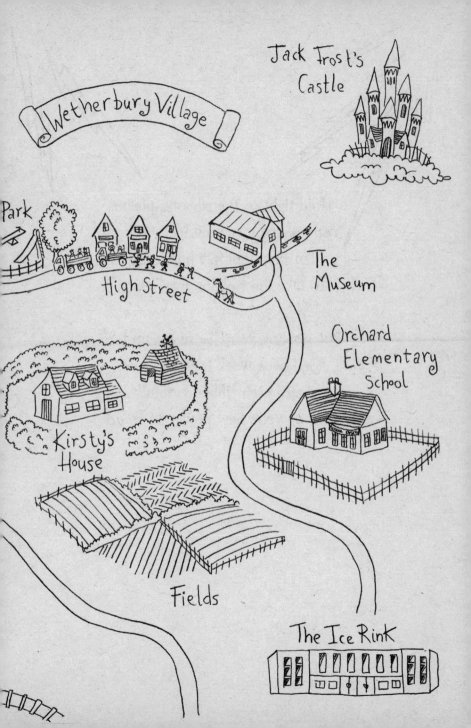

Hold tight to the ribbons, please.
You goblins may now feel a breeze.
I'm summoning a hurricane
To take the ribbons away again.

But, goblins, you'll be swept up too,
For I have work for you to do.
Guard each ribbon carefully,
By using your new power to freeze.

Contents

A Sparkling Skate   1

A Closet Full of Trouble   15

Team Goblin   23

Slipping and Sliding   31

Girls Net Goblins   49

A Magical Performance   59

A Sparkling Skate

"I can't wait to see the show!" Kirsty Tate told her best friend, Rachel Walker, as Mrs. Tate dropped the girls off outside the ice rink. After her mom promised to pick them up when the show was over, Kirsty exclaimed, "Oh, I just love ice dancing!"

"So do I," Rachel agreed.

"Good afternoon, ladies and gentlemen!" A voice boomed over the loudspeakers as the girls walked inside. "Welcome to the Glacier Ice Rink. We have a wonderful show for you today, so get ready to see all of your favorite fairy tale characters dancing on ice! The show begins in twenty minutes."

There was a long line of people

waiting to show their tickets, so the girls joined the line.

"I wish I could ice dance," Rachel said longingly. "I can skate pretty well, but I'd love to be able to do all those jumps and spins, and skate with a partner."

"Me, too!" Kirsty laughed. "My friend Jenny's playing Sleeping Beauty in the show today, and she's an amazing ice dancer! Even when she figure skates without a partner, she's really great. Let's go to the dressing rooms and wish her luck before the show starts."

Rachel nodded, but her expression was anxious. "Since Isabelle the Ice Dance Fairy's ribbon is still

missing, isn't Jenny's skating
going to be in danger?"

Kirsty nodded sadly. The
girls had spent their school
vacation trying to find the
Dance Fairies' seven magic
ribbons. Jack Frost had
stolen them, so he could use
their magic to make his clumsy goblins
dance well. The magic of the ribbons
helped make sure that dance
performances everywhere, including
Fairyland, went well and were fun for
everyone. Without the ribbons, dancing
went horribly wrong.

The king and queen of Fairyland had
demanded that the magic ribbons be
returned to the Dance Fairies, but Jack
Frost had cast a spell that sent seven of

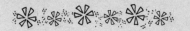

his goblins into the human world, each one clutching a ribbon that he would guard. The goblins were supposed to keep themselves and the ribbons hidden, but so far Rachel and Kirsty had managed to get six of the seven ribbons back.

"I'm just hoping the goblin with Isabelle's ribbon shows up at the ice rink today," Kirsty whispered as they handed in their tickets. "After all, each ribbon is

attracted to its own special type of
dance."

Rachel nodded. "I hope the goblin's
here somewhere, too," she replied.
"Mom and Dad are coming to take me
home tomorrow, so we have to find
Isabelle's ribbon before then."

The girls went into the auditorium.
The ice rink was surrounded by rows of

seats. Music was playing over the
loudspeakers as people began to sit down.

"Let's go and find Jenny," said Kirsty,
leading Rachel to the exit near the
dressing rooms.

As they entered the hallway, Rachel
gasped. She thought
she'd just seen
something green
disappear around
the corner at
the end of the hall.
Could it have been a
goblin? she wondered.

"What's the
matter, Rachel?"
Kirsty called, as
her friend ran
down the hallway.

Rachel stopped at the corner, looking all around, but there was no sign of goblins. "I thought I saw a goblin run around this corner!" she exclaimed, as Kirsty joined her. "But there's no one here."

"We've got goblins on the brain," Kirsty said, shaking her head. "Remember what Queen Titania said — we have to let the magic come to us!"

"Well, I hope it comes quickly," Rachel said with a sigh. "It would be great if we could find the missing ribbon before the show starts."

Kirsty and Rachel hurried to the dressing room where Jenny and the other

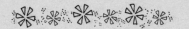

female skaters were getting ready. Jenny
was in front of a mirror, pinning her hair
up, when the girls came in. She smiled
at them.

"Hi, Jenny," Kirsty said cheerfully.
"This is my friend Rachel. We just came
to wish you luck."

"You look great, Jenny," Rachel said,
admiring her shimmering white dress.

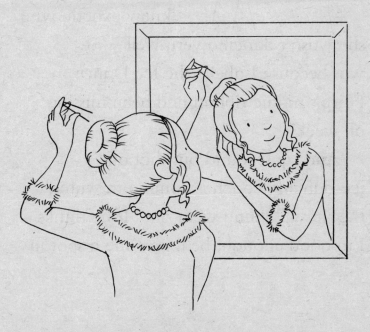

"Thanks," Jenny said. Then she looked down. "I really want to do well today, but I've been having trouble with my Sleeping Beauty routine recently. I just can't get my moves right!" Kirsty and Rachel felt sorry for Jenny. They knew exactly why she wasn't dancing very well — it was because Isabelle the Ice Dance Fairy's magic ribbon had been missing all week!

"And I just found out that an ice-dancing coach is coming to watch the show," Jenny went on. "If he thinks I'm good enough, he'll give me a spot in

the Ice Academy's summer school!" She
sighed. "I really want to go there, but if I
don't skate well today, I
won't even have a
chance!"

Rachel and Kirsty
glanced at each other
with concern. They
had to find Isabelle's
magic ribbon before
Jenny performed her
Sleeping Beauty routine.

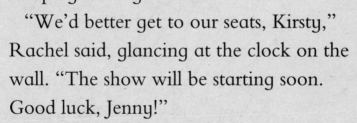

"We'd better get to our seats, Kirsty,"
Rachel said, glancing at the clock on the
wall. "The show will be starting soon.
Good luck, Jenny!"

"Yes, good luck!" Kirsty added.

"Thank you," Jenny said, pinning a

white flower into her hair. "Kirsty, could you hand me my ice skates, please?" she asked. "They're in the corner, just behind you."

"Sure," Kirsty said, turning around to get the skates. She stooped to pick them up, and her heart skipped a beat. One of

the skates was surrounded by a mist of blue glitter.

As she picked up the shimmering skate, a tiny fairy zoomed out of it in a burst of sparkles.

Kirsty recognized her immediately. "It's Isabelle the Ice Dance Fairy!" she whispered to herself with delight.

A Closet Full of Trouble

Isabelle hovered above the ice skate, waving up at Kirsty. She had long hair and wore a beautiful blue dress that was embroidered with silver sparkles. Tiny white ice skates glittered on her feet.

Kirsty quickly looked over her shoulder. Rachel was still chatting with Jenny, and

the other ice dancers were busy getting
ready. Nobody had noticed Isabelle.

"Hi, Kirsty," Isabelle whispered. "I
have good news. I can sense that my
magic ribbon is very close by!"

"Really?" Kirsty asked. "Let's start
looking for it right away!"

"I was hoping you'd say that," Isabelle
replied with a wink. Then she ducked
into Kirsty's pocket. Kirsty picked up the
other skate and carried it over to Jenny.

"Thanks," Jenny said, taking the skates and beginning to pull them on. "I wish I didn't feel so nervous!"

"Just do your best, Jenny," Kirsty said comfortingly. "Rachel and I will be cheering you on!"

Jenny nodded and began lacing up her pretty white skates as the girls left.

"Poor Jenny!" Rachel sighed as they walked along. "I wish we could help. But we don't even know whether the goblin with the ice dance ribbon is here or not."

"Oh, yes we do!" a silvery voice sang, and Isabelle peeked out of Kirsty's pocket. Kirsty couldn't help giggling at the look of surprise on Rachel's face.

"Hello, Isabelle!" Rachel laughed. "So your magic ribbon is here somewhere?"

Isabelle nodded. "We just have to find the goblin and get it back!"

"Oh!" Rachel exclaimed. "Kirsty, remember when I saw that flash of green on our way to find Jenny? Well, what if it was a goblin after all?"

"Let's go back and take another look," Kirsty suggested.

Quickly, they hurried back to the hallway where Rachel thought she'd seen the goblin. This time, as soon as they turned the corner, they saw a goblin a short way ahead of them. He was standing in front of a closet, pulling at the door handle.

"We found him!" Kirsty whispered as they came to a stop. "But I don't see the magic ribbon!"

The goblin hadn't noticed the girls
behind him, because he was too busy
tugging on the door. Just then, the door
flew open so suddenly that the goblin
fell over backward. Looking a little
embarrassed, he jumped to his feet and
then plunged into the closet. The door
slammed shut behind him. Rachel,
Kirsty, and Isabelle rushed after him.

"Don't forget that as long as the goblin has the magic ribbon, he also has the power to freeze things!" Isabelle warned, as Rachel reached for the door handle.

The girls nodded. Then, quickly, Rachel yanked the door open and looked inside. Immediately, she gave a gasp of horror, because inside the closet she could see not one goblin, but *seven*!

Team Goblin

For a moment Rachel, Kirsty, and Isabelle were too shocked to say anything. All three of them stared at the goblins, who were busy pulling on ice-hockey gear: helmets, red jerseys, elbow and knee pads, and ice skates.

Suddenly, one of the goblins looked up and spotted the girls. He gave a screech

of rage. "Go away!" he shrieked. "Don't you know it's rude to spy on people when they are getting dressed?" He reached out to try and pull the door closed, but Rachel firmly held onto it.

"Why are you putting on ice-hockey uniforms?" Rachel asked.

"Don't you know anything?" another goblin shouted back rudely. "These aren't ice-hockey outfits, they're ice-dance outfits!"

"Don't we look nice?" said a third goblin, and he began parading proudly up and down the hallway.

"But they're not ice-dance outfits," Rachel pointed out. "They're the uniforms for an ice-hockey team!"

The seven goblins looked confused and glanced at each other.

"Well, we don't care!" the biggest of the goblins snapped at last. "We're a team anyway — Team Goblin!"

"Yes, so go away and let us get dressed in peace!" shouted the first goblin. He tried to close the door again, but Rachel wouldn't let go.

"Listen, we'll leave you alone if you give us Isabelle's magic ribbon!" she said, but the goblins ignored her and kept dressing.

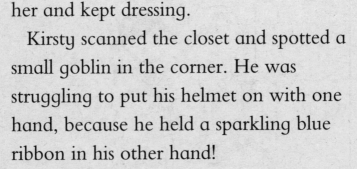

Kirsty scanned the closet and spotted a small goblin in the corner. He was struggling to put his helmet on with one hand, because he held a sparkling blue ribbon in his other hand!

"Look at that little goblin in the corner!" Kirsty whispered to her friends.

"He has my ribbon!" Isabelle declared, her eyes lighting up.

"How are we going to get it back?" Rachel asked urgently. "We need a plan!"

Just then, the biggest goblin turned to the goblin with the ribbon. "I'll hold that ribbon for you while you finish getting dressed," he offered with a sly smile.

"No, I'll hold it for you!" said another goblin, pushing the first one out of the way.

"Let me!" screeched a third, who was awkwardly hopping up and down in his skates. "I want to hold it!"

"No, me, me, me!" chorused the other goblins together.

"BE QUIET!" yelled the smallest goblin furiously. "NOBODY is going to hold the ribbon except ME!" He grinned smugly. "And now I'm off to dance on the ice!"

He dashed forward, slid through Rachel's legs, and ran down the hallway. Before the girls could figure out what to do, the six other goblins charged after him, knocking the girls aside.

"After him!" Isabelle yelled, and the three friends took off running.

The first goblin had danced his way along the hallway and was disappearing around the corner now. The others stumbled and tripped over their skates as they hurried after him.

"Come on!" Kirsty cried. "We have to keep the goblins from getting onto the ice, or everyone will see them!"

Slipping and Sliding

Kirsty, Rachel, and Isabelle rushed down
the hallway after the goblins. But as they
rounded the corner and the ice rink came
into view, Kirsty's heart sank. She could
see the smallest goblin zooming out onto
the ice, waving the ribbon joyfully in
one hand.

"This is awful!" Kirsty groaned as the other goblins followed their friend out onto the ice. "Everyone's going to see the goblins now, and we still don't have the ribbon!"

"We can't let them out of our sight," Isabelle whispered. "We might get a chance to grab the ribbon later." She hid in Rachel's pocket as the girls hurried to the edge of the rink.

The goblins were whooping with delight as they skated across the huge sheet of ice. As Rachel and Kirsty watched, they overheard a couple of women in the seats nearby, chatting to each other.

"I didn't know the junior ice-hockey team was part of today's show, did you?" the first woman asked. "That boy in front is such a talented skater!"

"Yes, but I thought the show was supposed to be about fairy tales!" the other woman replied, looking confused.

"At least the audience hasn't figured out that they're goblins!" Kirsty whispered to Rachel, relieved.

Music was still playing over the loudspeakers, and the small goblin with the ribbon began to dance in time to the beat. He glided expertly around the rink, performed a perfect spin, and then launched into a series

of spectacular jumps. The audience broke into a loud round of applause. The other goblins, who were skating in a long line, began trying to do the same moves. Rachel noticed that the goblin closest to the one with the ribbon managed to stay on his feet and even land some of the jumps, but the goblin at the end of the line could hardly stay upright, let alone dance. Rachel guessed it was because he was the farthest away from the ribbon and its dance magic.

Just then, the last goblin tried to jump
into the air, but slipped and fell! He went
skidding right across the ice and knocked
over the goblin in front of him. They
both ended up in a tangled heap.
The audience seemed to think it was
part of the show, and they laughed
and cheered.

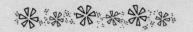

The goblin with the ribbon was still zooming around the rink, enjoying the applause. He passed the last goblin in the line, just as the goblin was struggling to his feet. The last goblin's eyes lit up as he spotted the ribbon flash by him, and he made a determined lunge for it. But the goblin with the ribbon easily dodged him and skated to the edge of the ice. There, he ran through the gate at the far side of the rink.

"Let's run around and see if we can head him off!" Kirsty suggested.

The girls took off, racing around the rink. But by the time they reached the other gate, the last of the goblins had already scrambled off the ice. He stuck

his tongue out at Rachel and Kirsty, and dashed off after the others, who were clattering down the hallway on their skates.

"There's another rink at the end of this hall." Kirsty panted as the three friends raced after the goblins. "I think it's where the ice-hockey team practices."

The girls sighed with frustration as they saw the goblins skate onto the ice again.

This rink was smaller than the main one
and had ice-hockey nets at each end.
Once on the ice, the goblin with the
ribbon began to dance beautifully,
leaping and spinning on the thin skate
blades, while the others tried in vain to
keep up with him.

"We need to get onto the ice and grab
that ribbon!" Rachel said.

"For that, you'll need skates!" Isabelle declared, and with a flick of her wand, the girls' shoes vanished and were replaced with snow-white ice skates. The goblin with the ribbon whizzed around the rink, and Rachel and Kirsty waited until he was near the gate where they stood. Then they glided out to try and snatch the ribbon away from him. Unfortunately, the goblin was too fast, so the girls had to skate quickly after him, with Isabelle flying alongside. Just behind them were the six other goblins, still trying to keep up with their friend.

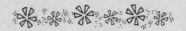

"Look out!" shouted one of the goblins behind them. "Those pesky girls are getting close!"

The goblin with the ribbon glanced over his shoulder, alarmed to see how close Rachel and Kirsty were. He sped up and started dodging from side to side, so that the girls couldn't catch him. Rachel and Kirsty skated faster too, pulling away from the other goblins.

With the magic of the ribbon getting farther away, the other goblins began to stumble and bump into one another. Suddenly, the goblin at the front of the line fell backward with a loud shriek. He knocked into the goblin behind him, who bumped into the goblin behind him, and all the goblins fell over, one by one, like a row of dominoes. They lay on the ice groaning and blaming one another.

"Stop fighting!" the goblin with the ribbon shouted, skating toward his friends. "We have to stick together to protect the ribbon from those pesky girls! Imagine how angry Jack Frost will be if we come back without any ribbons at all!"

The goblins stopped arguing at once.

"That's true!" one goblin said thoughtfully. "Those girls are sneaky. They dropped a moon on my head to get my ribbon!"

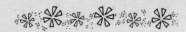

"Yes," agreed the one with the very pointy nose. "They made me fall into a swimming pool!"

"Well, they bowled me over with a disco ball," another goblin added angrily.

"And now they're trying to take *my* ribbon!" the ribbon-holding goblin yelled.

All seven goblins glared at Rachel and Kirsty. "I think it's time to make some girl popsicles!" the biggest goblin called, as the goblins untangled themselves and staggered to their feet.

"Ooh, yes!" the goblin with the ribbon said excitedly, stopping beside his friends. "I'd forgotten I could do that!"

"Watch out, girls!" Isabelle cried. "They're after *us* now!"

Rachel and Kirsty took off across the ice as the seven goblins linked hands and zoomed after them.

"We're right behind you!" the goblin with the ribbon yelled.

"Freeze them! Freeze them!" the other goblins chanted.

Rachel and Kirsty headed for the exit from the rink, but the goblins skated over to block their path. The girls glanced at each other in desperation. They were trapped!

"Girls!" Isabelle called, waving her wand over Rachel and Kirsty's heads. "Fly up to me!"

Just then, the ribbon-holding goblin whizzed toward the girls, shouting "FREEEEEZE!" And at the same moment, Rachel and Kirsty found themselves surrounded by a cloud of blue fairy magic. Soon they were fairy-size

with delicate fairy wings. The girls
zipped upward to join Isabelle.

"Come back!" the goblin yelled. "I
want to freeze you!" He leaped high into
the air. To the goblin's disappointment,
his outstretched fingers just missed
the girls.

"Please take your seats," a voice
announced over the loudspeaker. "The
show will start in three minutes."

"The show is about to begin!" Kirsty
gasped. "Jenny will be on the ice soon.
We have to get the ribbon back!"

Girls Net Goblins

Rachel glanced around desperately, and her gaze fell on one of the hockey nets. "I've got an idea!" she exclaimed, pointing to the hockey goal. "Isabelle, when I give you a signal, can you use your magic to make that net tip over?"

Isabelle nodded, then whirled off to position herself above the net.

"Follow me, Kirsty," Rachel whispered.

Kirsty nodded and grinned. She thought she had a pretty good idea what her friend was planning.

Rachel and Kirsty flew down and hovered just above the goblins, being careful to stay away from the one with the ribbon.

"You can't catch me!" Rachel cried.

"Or me!" Kirsty added.

The goblins looked furious. All seven of them dashed forward, desperately trying to grab Kirsty and Rachel. The girls fluttered just out of the goblins' reach, staying close enough that the goblins kept jumping up and trying to catch them. Little by little, the girls flew over to the hockey net where Isabelle was waiting.

"Quick, Kirsty!" Rachel whispered. "Into the net!"

The two girls

flew right into the net, and the goblins
followed without even a pause.

"NOW, Isabelle!" Rachel
cried.

A cloud of sparkling
fairy dust burst from
Isabelle's wand and
made the net tip
right over. It fell on
top of the goblins,
trapping them like a
cage. Rachel and
Kirsty were small
enough to slip
through the netting
and fly up to join
Isabelle.

"Let us go!" the goblins
yelled angrily, pushing and

shoving at the net. But there was no
way out. The net was too heavy
for them to lift. Just
then, Kirsty caught a
glimpse of something
blue sparkling in the
middle of the tangle
of goblin arms and
legs. She flew down,
slipped her hand
through the netting,
and pulled the
magic ribbon free.
Isabelle clapped her
hands in delight as
Kirsty handed the
ribbon back to her.
The fairy quickly
reattached the ribbon

to her wand and, as she did, it shimmered a beautiful, deep blue. "My ribbon is safe at last!" Isabelle sighed happily as the three of them flew over to the side of the rink. "All the Dance Fairies have their dance ribbons again, and it's thanks to you, girls. Now you should go and watch Jenny perform. I'll clean up here."

She waved her wand, and Rachel and Kirsty were instantly back to their normal size again, wearing their normal shoes. They watched as Isabelle's magic then lifted the net upright, freeing

the goblins. They got to their feet, grumbling.

"Let's get out of here!" one mumbled, and they began to skate off gloomily. But without the magic of the ribbon to help them, they kept slipping and sliding everywhere!

"Stop!" Isabelle called suddenly. "You're not going anywhere with that hockey gear on!" With another wave of her wand, the ice-hockey uniforms fell off the goblins and clattered onto the ice.

The goblins scowled as they scrambled off the ice without any skates, complaining loudly about their cold feet.

"Girls, I need to go and give everyone in Fairyland the good news!" Isabelle declared. "But don't worry, you'll see the Dance Fairies again — maybe sooner than you think!" She flicked her wand and had just enough time to wave

good-bye before a shower of blue
sparkles whisked her off to Fairyland.

"We did it, Kirsty!" Rachel beamed as
they ran back to the main ice rink. "We
found all seven dance ribbons!"

Kirsty was smiling, too. "Every kind of
dancing should go well now — including
ice dance! Let's go and cheer Jenny on!"

A Magical Performance

"Jenny's just spectacular!" Kirsty whispered to Rachel, as Jenny took off for yet another amazing jump. She landed perfectly on the ice and then went into a fast spin. The audience clapped, and Kirsty and Rachel joined in enthusiastically.

"She's great!" Rachel gasped as the music finished and Jenny took a bow.

Kirsty grinned. "At intermission, we should go and tell her that!" she suggested.

After watching Red Riding Hood and the Wolf, followed by Cinderella and her Ugly Stepsisters, it was time for intermission. Rachel and Kirsty hurried off to see Jenny. They found her in the dressing room, hanging up her skates.

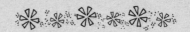

"Oh, you'll never guess what just happened!" she exclaimed when she saw Rachel and Kirsty. "I was just offered a spot in the Ice Academy's summer school! They told me as soon as I came off the ice."

"I'm not surprised," Kirsty said happily as Jenny beamed at them. "You were fantastic!"

"And the whole show is going so well!" Rachel said, smiling.

"Everyone seems to be skating much better today," Jenny said. "I'll come and watch the rest of the show with you after I've changed."

Rachel and Kirsty nodded and left the dressing room to go back to their seats.

"I wonder what Isabelle meant when she said we'd see the Dance Fairies again sooner than we might think," Rachel remarked thoughtfully, as Kirsty stopped at a vending machine to get a drink.

As Kirsty pressed the button, the

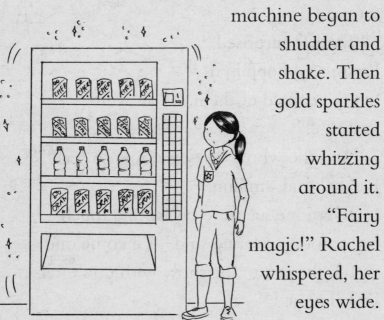

machine began to shudder and shake. Then gold sparkles started whizzing around it. "Fairy magic!" Rachel whispered, her eyes wide.

The girls watched in amazement as
a golden envelope fell into the tray at
the bottom of the machine, followed
by Kirsty's can of juice.

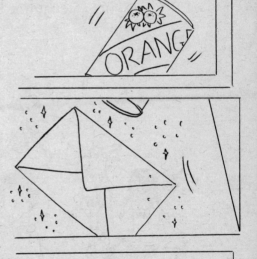

Kirsty sprang
forward, put her
hand through the
flap, and picked
up the envelope.

"It has our
names on it!" she
said, amazed.

"Open it!"
Rachel urged.

As Kirsty opened
the envelope, a rainbow of bright colors
burst from it. In the middle of the colors,
a face began to appear.

"It's Queen Titania!" Rachel gasped.

x

"And look!" Kirsty laughed. "There are the Dance Fairies, too!"

The queen smiled as the Dance Fairies fluttered around her, waving happily at Rachel and Kirsty.

"Girls, you've helped us once again,"

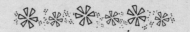

she announced. "In return, we would like to invite you to Fairyland for a day of dance with the Dance Fairies."

"Ooh, we'd love that!" Rachel and Kirsty chorused.

"Then we'll come and get you very soon!" The queen laughed. "And thank you!"

The queen and the Dance Fairies disappeared in a shimmering burst of color, and Kirsty and Rachel gazed at each other in delight.

"I can't wait!" Rachel said, her eyes shining. "It's going to be so much fun to learn all the different kinds of dance!"

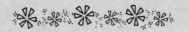

Kirsty grinned. "We've had some great fairy adventures together, haven't we?" she said.

Rachel nodded. "And I have a feeling that this one won't be our last!" she said happily.

THE Music FAIRIES

The Dance Fairies all have their magic
ribbons back, but now another group of
fairies is in trouble! Can Rachel and
Kirsty help the Music Fairies, too?
Don't miss

Poppy
the Piano Fairy!

Check out the girls' next adventure in
this special sneak peek!

A Musical Message

"Ooh, I love to dance!" Rachel Walker sang along to the radio, pretending her hairbrush was a microphone. "When I hear the music, my toes start tapping and my fingers start snapping!"

Kirsty Tate, Rachel's best friend, grinned and grabbed her own hairbrush.

"I can't stop dancing!" she chorused.

The girls tried to do a complicated dance routine as they sang, but then Kirsty went left and Rachel went right. They ended up bumping into each other! Laughing, they collapsed onto Kirsty's bedroom carpet.

"I don't think we'd be very good in a band, Rachel!" Kirsty said, giggling.

"That was The Sparkle Girls with their new single, *Can't Stop Dancing*," the radio DJ announced as Kirsty and Rachel sat up. "If anyone out there thinks they could make it big as a pop star, too, why not audition for the National Talent Competition next weekend?"

"That sounds cool!" Rachel said.

"One lucky singer or band will win a recording contract with MegaBig Records," the DJ went on. "So remember — come to the New Harmony Mall next weekend, and maybe one day I'll be playing *your* songs on my show!"

"The New Harmony Mall is only a few miles from Wetherbury," Kirsty said dreamily. "I'm sure Mom or Dad would take us to watch the competition if we asked them."

Just then, a tiny, silvery voice sang from the radio. "Kirsty and Rachel!" it called. "Can you hear me, girls?"

Was it a fairy?

There's Magic in Every Book!

The Rainbow Fairies
Books #1-7

The Weather Fairies
Books #1-7

The Jewel Fairies
Books #1-7

The Pet Fairies
Books #1-7

The Fun Day Fairies
Books #1-7

◼SCHOLASTIC
www.scholastic.com
www.rainbowmagiconline.com

HIT entertainment

FAIRYG